Zeke Meeks

McNUTTY
SMARTY PANTS
POOPSTER
EVIL NAILS
BEST FRIEND
SCARY!!!
Snow White
LA-LA-LA
THRILLSVILLE!
EPIC
THE EMMAS
I RULE
SING-A-LONG
BUG TRAINER
EWW
RIP
ME

Sugar, a.k.a. - the best
thing ever invented.

Zeke Meeks is published by
Picture Window Books,
A Capstone Imprint
1710 Roe Crest Drive
North Mankato, Minnesota 56003
www.capstonepub.com

Copyright © 2015 Picture Window Books

Library of Congress Cataloging-in-Publication Data
Green, D. L. (Debra L.), author.
    Zeke Meeks vs the Mother's Day meltdown / by D.L. Green; illustrated by Josh Alves.
        pages cm. — (Zeke Meeks)
    Summary: Annoyed because his mother has been packing boring, healthy lunches, third-
grader Zeke has not made either a card or a gift for Mother's Day — then at the last
moment he has a change of heart and has to scramble to make both.
    ISBN 978-1-4795-2168-5 (hardcover)
    ISBN 978-1-4795-5769-1 (pbk.)
    ISBN 978-1-4795-6209-1 (ebook)
1. Mother's Day—Juvenile fiction. 2. Middle-born children—Juvenile fiction. 3. Brothers
and sisters—Juvenile fiction. 4. Mothers and sons—Juvenile fiction. 5. Elementary schools—
Juvenile fiction. [1. Mother's Day—Fiction. 2. Schools—Fiction. 3. Humorous stories.] I. Alves,
Josh, illustrator. II. Title. III. Title: Zeke Meeks versus the Mother's Day meltdown. IV.
Series: Green, D. L. (Debra L.) Zeke Meeks.

    PZ7.G81926Zg 2015
    813.6—dc23   2014022383

Vector Credits: Shutterstock
Book design by: Kristi Carlson

Printed in China.
092014   008472RRDS15

Pickles - __NOT__ the best
thing ever invented.

Zeke Meeks

VS THE MOTHER'S DAY MELTDOWN

BY D. L. GREEN

ILLUSTRATED BY JOSH ALVES

UN-HAPPY MOTHER'S DAY

PICTURE WINDOW BOOKS

a capstone imprint

TABLE OF

This is 100% true. Okay,
it's not. But it should be.

:(Total failure.

BOYS RULE EVERYTHING BUT THE PLAYGROUND

Something so gross,
not even Waggles
will eat it.

Waffles are delicious and easy to make, right? WRONG.

CONTENTS

Totally doesn't exist.

Princess Sing-Along doesn't exist either. Thank goodness.

GIRLS DROOL ALL BUT GRACE — SHE BITES

The Only Thing MORE BORING than Celery Sticks Is NOTHING

Maybe.

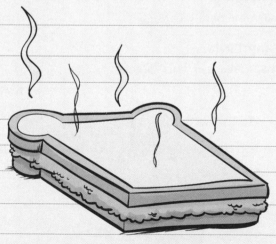

Eww. Mom had made me a tuna fish sandwich. The bread was soggy and the tuna fish smelled awful, like fish.

I reached into my lunchbox to see what else my mom had packed. Celery sticks. Yuck. Whole-grain crackers. Ho hum. A thermos of milk. Yawn. That was all. I probably had the worst lunch in the whole, entire third grade.

Danny Ford, who sat next to me at the lunch table, peered at my sandwich and said, "Zeke, your tuna fish smells fishy." Then he laughed and said, "Get it? Get it?"

I rolled my eyes. The sandwich was bad enough. I didn't need a bad joke too.

"The joke is that tuna fish smells fishy. Get it?"

"I get the joke. But I don't think it's funny. Not at all," I said.

I looked at Danny's lunch and licked my lips. He had a huge slice of pizza dripping with cheese, three big chocolate chip cookies, and a giant caramel apple. I asked him, "Do you want to trade anything?"

Danny glanced at my lunch and made a face.

"Does that mean yes, you want to trade?" I asked.

"No," Danny said.

"You don't want crunchy, fun celery sticks?" I asked.

He shook his head.

"How about a huge mound of crackers?" I asked.

"What kind of crackers?" he asked.

"The tasty kind," I lied.

Owen Leach pointed at my crackers from across the table. "I saw those at the store. They're salt-free and baked instead of fried. I bet they taste like old cardboard. Yuck."

"They don't taste like old cardboard," I said.

They tasted more like new cardboard. I knew that because my cousin once gave me a dollar to eat a piece of cardboard. It tasted terrible.

Owen opened his bag of potato chips. "Too bad your mom is awful at packing lunch, Zeke."

I didn't like hearing other people insult my mom. I said, "My mom is good in other ways. She let me watch a TV show yesterday after I did my homework and chores."

"You only got to see one little TV show? And you had to do homework and chores first? Your mom is mean. My mom lets me watch TV whenever I want," Owen said.

"I stay up really late most nights watching TV in my bedroom," Danny said.

I didn't have a TV in my bedroom. I had to share the TV in the living room with my whole, entire family.

"When I'm at my dad and stepmom's house, I watch TV in my bedroom there, too," Danny said.

"You're lucky," I said.

"I didn't have time to watch TV last weekend," Laurie Schneider said.

"Were you busy doing homework and chores?" I asked.

"No. My grandma took me fishing at the lake."

I stared at Laurie across the table. Actually, I stared at the big chocolate cupcake in front of her.

Then I asked, "Want to trade something for that cupcake? My crunchy, yummy celery sticks? A big pile of crackers that honestly don't taste like old cardboard? A tuna fish sandwich that's full of fresh flavor?"

Laurie shook her head. "No, no, and no. Gross. Besides, if I want tuna fish or any other fish, I can catch it myself next time my grandma takes me to the lake."

Grace Chang leaned across the table and waved a donut in my face. The donut was covered with thick, chocolate frosting.

I licked my lips again.

"Hey, Zeke the Freak. Do you want to trade your celery sticks for my donut?" Grace asked.

"Yes. Thank you," I said.

"I bet you do. But I don't want to trade. No way." Grace laughed her evil laugh. "Ba-ha-ha-ha."

Next to her, Emma G. laughed too. "Ba-ha-ha-ha." She tried to sound evil, but she just sounded silly.

Next to Emma G., Emma J. laughed too. "Ba-ha-ha-ha." She sounded silly too.

"Hey, Zeke the Freak. Maybe one day your mom will be nice and pack you a good lunch," Grace said. "But I doubt it."

"Yeah. I doubt it," Emma G. said.

"Yeah. I doubt it," Emma J. said.

I doubted it too.

I sighed and took a bite of my tuna fish sandwich. It smelled really fishy, but I was really hungry. So I plugged my nose and finished eating it.

Danny licked chocolate chip cookie crumbs from his lips and said, "*Mmm*. My mom makes the best cookies. I should get her something special for Mother's Day. She deserves it. I should get my stepmom something special too. She deserves it, too."

"*Mah muh her duh zuh hum hee speh hul fo Muh her Day*," Owen said with his mouth full of potato chips.

"What did you say?" I asked.

Owen finished his chips and said, "My mother deserves something special for Mother's Day too."

Laurie licked the frosting off her cupcake and said, "So does my grandma."

I stared at my awful lunch. Then I thought
about all of my mom's rules and all the chores
I had to do. The more I thought about it, the
more it seemed like my mom didn't deserve
anything for Mother's Day. Except maybe some
boring celery sticks and fishy tuna fish.

When I got home from school, I smelled an awesome aroma. I followed the scent into the kitchen.

Mmm. Two large plates of warm chocolate-marshmallow-caramel brownies sat on the counter. I reached out to take one.

Mom grabbed my hand before it reached the brownies. She said, "I made those for your sister's preschool bake sale. Don't eat them."

"But they look so good, and I'm so hungry," I said.

"Don't worry. I made brownies for our family too," Mom said.

I licked my lips.

Mom brought over a plate of brownies. They didn't have an awesome aroma. They didn't even smell good.

They were not warm either. And they didn't have chocolate or marshmallow or caramel in them. They weren't even brown. The brownies for our family were beige and plain.

Maybe they tasted yummy anyway. Some beige, plain things did. Pecan ice cream, potato chips, and buttered noodles were all beige and plain *and* yummy.

I grabbed a beige, plain brownie and bit into it.

Ugh. I spit the piece of brownie into my hand.

"Don't you like it? It's a sugarless oat-wheat-bran brownie. It's good for you," Mom said.

IT TASTES GOOD <u>FOR</u> ME. BUT IT DOESN'T TASTE GOOD.

My little sister, Mia, walked into the kitchen. She said, "That reminds me of a song."

I groaned. "Oh, no. Not a Princess Sing-Along Song."

Princess Sing-Along was a pretend princess on TV who sang awful songs in a screechy voice.

"You're wrong, Zeke. It *is* a Princess Sing-Along Song," Mia said. Then she sang in her screechy voice, "Don't eat too much sugar, please, la la la. It can give you a disease, la la la. Sugar can make your heart quiver, la la la. And it can damage your liver, la la la."

I pointed to the sugarless oat-wheat-bran brownies. "Brownies without sugar are awful. I won't eat them. If I don't eat, I'll starve and die. Dying is worse than having a quivering heart or a damaged liver. So sugar is actually good for me. It keeps me alive," I said.

"That doesn't make any sense," Mom said.

Maybe it didn't. But sugarless brownies didn't make any sense either. I bet Danny's mother and stepmother let him eat brownies full of sugar all day long. Maybe they even poured sugar right into his mouth. Danny was probably in his bedroom right now, eating yummy, sugary brownies while he watched TV.

"Mom, can I have a TV in my bedroom?" I asked.

"No. You can use the TV in the living room," she said.

I walked toward the living room.

"First, do your homework, clean your room, and feed the dog," she added.

"And wait until my TV show is over. It's about the most romantic love scenes of all time," my older sister, Alexa, said.

Yuck. I bet Danny never had to wait until his sister's TV show was over. I bet he didn't even have a sister. I said, "Mom, my friends at school have TVs in their bedrooms. And they eat junk food for lunch and go to fun places."

"We go to fun places," Mom said.

This week, Mom had taken me to school, the dentist, and the grocery store. None of those places were fun. Laurie's grandma took her fishing at the lake. That sounded like a lot of fun.

"Mom, can you take me fishing at the lake?" I asked.

She shook her head. "I don't like fishing. Maybe your dad will take you fishing when he comes home."

I sighed. My dad was a soldier, far away on a top-secret mission. We didn't know when he'd come home. It could be months from now.

"Instead of fishing, I'll take you shopping at the discount store. You need new underwear and socks," Mom said.

I sighed again. Shopping for underwear and socks wasn't fun at all.

"Zeke, you just reminded me of a Princess Sing-Along song," Mia said.

I sighed again. I said, "Don't sing any more Prin—"

It was too late. Mia sang in her screechy voice, "If you sunbathe at a lake, la la la, wear sunblock for goodness sake, la la la. Also beware of poison oak, la la la. Itchy, scaly skin is no joke, la la la."

Mom smiled. "Some of those Princess Sing-Along songs are great."

I didn't think any of those songs were great. I didn't even think they were good. Listening to them made me mad.

Other things that made me mad were bad lunches, sugarless brownies, sharing the TV, shopping for socks and underwear, and my mom.

My mom made me maddest of all.

Something VERY SPECIAL and SWEET and the OPPOSITE of GREAT

Soooo not great.

Things did not improve the next day.

Worst things about my morning:

1. I had forgotten to study for the spelling test.

2. I failed the spelling test.

3. My teacher, Mr. McNutty, gave a boring grammar lesson.

4. I fell asleep during the boring grammar lesson.

5. My classmates laughed at me for falling asleep.

Worst things about lunchtime:

1. My mom had packed me an apple.

2. Owen's mom packed him a big slice of apple pie.

3. Owen wouldn't trade his slice of apple pie for my apple.

4. Owen wouldn't even trade half his slice of apple pie for my whole, entire apple.

5. Owen wouldn't even trade one tiny bite of his slice of apple pie for my whole, entire apple.

I hoped things would get better in the afternoon. They couldn't get much worse.

After lunch, Mr. McNutty told the class, "Are you ready for something very special and sweet?"

"Yeah! I'm very ready!" I said.

My classmates were ready too. Owen Leach said, "Bring it on!"

Victoria Crow said, "I welcome the opportunity."

Aaron Glass said, "I have to go to the bathroom."

Okay, he wasn't ready.

After Aaron was back from using the bathroom, Mr. McNutty said, "To prepare for this very special and sweet thing, you must clean the tops of your desks."

I bet we needed room on our desks for a very special and sweet snack. I licked my lips. I wondered whether the snack was cupcakes, cookies, or ice cream. Maybe it was cupcakes *and* cookies *and* ice cream.

I cleared the top of my desk. There were a lot of things on it:

1. Pencils, a ruler, and other boring school supplies.

2. Rocks I'd found on the playground.

3. A note from my best friend, Hector, saying hi.

4. A note from my second best friend, Charlie, asking what Hector's note said.

5. A second note from Hector, asking what Charlie's note said.

6. A second note from Charlie, asking what Hector's second note said.

7. A note from Rudy Morse, who sat next to me, saying he was tired of passing me notes.

Once everyone had cleared their desks, Mr. McNutty said, "It looks like you're ready for something very special and sweet. Try not to make a mess. I don't want your desks to get white and sticky."

What very special and sweet thing was white and sticky? Marshmallows? Glazed donuts? Vanilla frosting? Maybe we'd get to eat all three. I licked my lips again.

Then I raised my hand and said, "Don't worry, Mr. McNutty. I won't leave a white and sticky mess. I'll eat everything."

ZEKE, DON'T JOKE AROUND. EATING GLUE COULD MAKE YOU SICK.

Glue? I didn't want to eat glue. I wanted marshmallows, glazed donuts, and vanilla frosting.

"This is the very special, sweet thing," said Mr. McNutty. He held up a piece of thick white paper with a pretend bug on it.

Yikes! That wasn't very special or sweet. It was very scary and horrible. I was terrified of bugs. Not just big, ugly bugs. I was terrified of all bugs. I was even terrified of pictures of bugs.

"You'll be making Mother's Day cards," said Mr. McNutty. He passed out thick white paper, colored paper cut into circles for the bug's body, colored paper shaped like cones for the bug's wings, googly eyes, and pipe cleaners for the bug's antennae. Yikes.

Mr. McNutty told us to fold the thick, white paper in half to make the card. Then we had to glue everything onto the front of the card to make a bug and then decorate it with markers. On the inside of the card, we were supposed to write, "Happy Mother's Day from your love bug." Yuck.

"Aww! That's sweet. I'll make a love bug card for my grandmother," Laurie said.

"I told you it was sweet. And very special too," Mr. McNutty said. "Be careful with the white, sticky glue. Don't eat it, Zeke."

The class laughed.

I frowned.

Danny raised his hand. "May I make one card for my mother and one for my stepmother?"

"Of course," Mr. McNutty said.

I raised my hand. "Does everyone have to make a card?"

"Yes," my teacher said. "It's a nice way to thank your mothers and grandmothers and stepmothers for all the great things they've done for you."

My mother hadn't done great things for me. She hadn't taken me fishing or bought me a TV for my bedroom. She mostly just made me do homework and chores. That wasn't great. It was the opposite of great. It was un-great or non-great or great-less or whatever the word was. I didn't want to make a bug card for my mother. I didn't want to make anything for my mother.

My classmates got to work.

I goofed off. I glued my fingers together. I made weird creatures out of the pipe cleaners. I balled up the colored paper. I didn't write "Happy Mother's Day from your love bug." Instead, I wrote, "The only thing worse than a bug is my mother." Then I glued the weird pipe cleaner creatures and balls of paper to the front of the card.

Luckily, Mr. McNutty didn't notice what I was doing. He also didn't notice that I'd gotten my desk full of white, sticky glue.

Roses Are RED, Violets Are BLUE,

1 tasty cookie
+ 1 side of guilt
‾‾‾‾‾‾‾‾‾‾‾‾‾‾
= 1 sad lunch

Cookies Are SWEET, I AM NOT.

The next day at lunchtime, I sat next to
Danny again. I wondered what his mother had
packed for him. A cheeseburger? Cotton candy?
Chocolate-covered pretzels? Danny was so
lucky.

I opened my lunchbox and took out a
boring turkey sandwich and a boring peeled
orange. I had the worst mom in the whole,
entire school. I only felt a tiny bit guilty about
not making her a Mother's Day card.

I spotted something under the boring food in my lunchbox. I picked it up. Wow! It was a bag full of cookies.

I opened the bag and sniffed the cookies. *Mmm!*

Then I shoved them in my mouth. The mixture of chocolate, sugar, and butter tasted amazing.

After I finished the cookies and licked the crumbs around my mouth, I saw a note in my lunchbox.

I did not feel sweet. I felt un-sweet or non-sweet or sweet-less or whatever the word was. And I felt a little guilty about not making a Mother's Day card.

"Those cookies looked good. You're so lucky, Zeke," Danny said. He opened his lunch box. He took out a cheese sandwich on brown, grainy bread, a large carrot, and an orange with its peel still on.

I was so shocked, my mouth dropped open.

I closed my mouth and asked, "What happened, Danny? I haven't seen you eat healthy food all week."

Danny frowned. "My mom found out I was packing junk food for lunch."

My mouth dropped again.

I closed it again and asked, "You pack your own lunches?"

"Yeah. Ever since I started third grade. My mom said I was old enough to do it."

I was in third grade too. I was glad my mom didn't make me pack my own lunch.

Danny pointed to my orange. "How long did it take you to peel that?"

"No time at all. My mom peeled it," I said.

"Your mom packed your lunch and peeled your orange for you? You're so lucky," Danny said again.

"I thought you were lucky because you ate junk food for lunch," I said.

He sighed. "My mom didn't know I was packing junk food. When she found out, she got really mad. Now I have to pack healthy stuff. And to make up for my unhealthy lunches, I'm not allowed to eat any junk food for the rest of the month. Also, my mom took away my TV."

My mom wasn't the worst mom of the whole, entire school. Danny's mother was. I felt even guiltier about not making my mom a card.

I told Danny, "I bet you're so mad at your mom now. You probably won't even give her a Mother's Day card."

"Of course I'll give her a card. And a gift," Danny said. "I saved my allowance money for two months so I could buy my mother a nice bottle of perfume."

That made me feel even guiltier. I'd spent all my allowance money on candy, trading cards, and video games. I hadn't bought anything for my mom.

"I'm giving my grandma a fishing trip," Laurie said. "We'll spend Mother's Day at the lake."

"That's more of a gift for you than for her," I said.

Laurie shook her head. "I don't like fishing at all. Last time I went, I spent four long hours next to a fishing pole. Guess what I caught."

"Fish," I said.

"Only one fish. I got only one single, small, slimy, smelly fish. I also got itchy mosquito bites and a bright red sunburn. My grandma forgot to bring the bug spray and sunblock."

My mom never forgot bug spray and sunblock. She was a good mom. I felt very guilty for not making her a card or getting her a gift.

Mother's Day was only three days away. Too bad I didn't have any money saved for a present. Or a way to get to a store. Or knew how to make a gift. Or had many craft supplies. It was really too bad that I'd goofed off instead of making my mom a Mother's Day card. I felt extremely guilty.

In a Pickle

A very, very, smelly pickle.

When I got home from school, my mom said, "I feel guilty."

I was the one who should have been feeling guilty. I had nothing to give Mom for Mother's Day.

Mom had no reason to feel guilty. She always gave me presents on my birthday and Christmas. If there were a holiday called Son Day, she'd give me presents for that too.

"I feel guilty because I told you I wouldn't take you fishing," Mom said.

After hearing Laurie Schneider complain about fishing, I no longer wanted to go. I didn't want to spend four boring hours catching one tiny fish. I didn't want a bright red sunburn. And I really didn't want to be bitten by scary mosquitos. I didn't want to be anywhere near scary mosquitos.

"Zeke, you deserve to fish in the lake," Mom said.

I didn't deserve to fish in the lake. I deserved to be thrown in the lake. I was the worst son in the whole, entire world. I had to give Mom something for Mother's Day.

I sat at the computer and searched the Internet for a present I could make. Most of the crafts seemed too hard or listed supplies we didn't have.

I finally found a pretty vase that I thought
Mom would like. It looked easy to make. I just
needed scissors, glue, tissue paper, and a jar. We
had the first three things in my mom's office.

I went to the kitchen and looked for a jar. I
didn't find any in the cupboards.

"What are you doing?" Mom asked me.

"Um . . . uh . . . well . . . " I couldn't tell Mom about her gift, so I lied. "I'm testing the cupboard doors to make sure they open and close okay."

Mom raised her eyebrows. That meant she didn't believe me.

I searched for a jar in the refrigerator.

"Now what are you doing?" Mom asked me.

"Um . . . uh . . . well . . . I'm looking for something to eat."

Aha! I spotted a pickle jar on the bottom shelf of the fridge. It had three pickles in it. Once they were eaten, I could use the jar. I took it out of the fridge.

"I thought you didn't like pickles," Mom said.

"I changed my mind." I sat at the kitchen table and opened the jar. *Ugh.* Pickles smelled gross.

I took out a pickle. *Ugh.* It was green and bumpy and smelly.

I whistled softly for our dog.

Waggles came over right away. I held the pickle under the table for Waggles to eat. He always ate everything.

He sniffed the pickle. Then he whimpered and ran away.

I was wrong. Waggles always ate everything except pickles.

Mom brought over two plates and sat at the table with me.

I put the green, bumpy, smelly pickle on a plate. *Ugh.*

Mia came into the kitchen and said, "Princess Sing-Along would be proud of you for trying new foods, Zeke." Before I could stop her, Mia screeched a Princess Sing-Along song: "Don't be scared to try new things, la la la. Like spinach and lima beans, la la la. Though after you chew them up, la la la, you may want to spew them up, la la la."

That song was almost as gross as pickles. I didn't tell Mia that. Instead, I said, "Try some pickles, Mia. They're yummy."

"*Eww.* No way," Mia said.

"Alexa!" I called out. "Do you want a delicious pickle?"

"There's no such thing as a delicious pickle! Pickles are disgusting!" Alexa yelled back.

"Zeke, I thought you wanted to eat a pickle," Mom said.

I wished Mom would leave the kitchen. Then I could throw away the pickles and take the jar. But she stayed at the kitchen table.

So I ate the pickle. It tasted horrible.

I pulled another pickle out of the jar and ate that one, too. *Ugh.*

"Mom, these pickles are great. Try one," I said.

Luckily, she did. The pickle jar was finally empty. Unluckily, Mom threw the jar into the kitchen trash can. Luckily, she went to the bathroom.

I dug the empty pickle jar out of the trash. The jar had big, brown coffee grounds stuck to it. It smelled like a horrible mixture of sour pickles and old coffee.

I rinsed the jar in the kitchen sink with soap and water. But I couldn't get rid of the sour pickle/old coffee stink.

Then I carried the jar to my bedroom and closed the door.

Next I got scissors, glue, and tissue paper from my mom's office. I wasn't supposed to use scissors or glue in my bedroom.

I took them to my room anyway.

I cut the tissue paper into squares. Then I covered the pickle jar with glue.

Just as I was about to glue the tissue paper squares on the jar, someone knocked on my bedroom door.

"Who is it?" I asked.

"Your mother. I'm coming in."

"Wait!" I yelled. I couldn't let her see her gift or the scissors or glue.

She didn't wait. She started opening my door.

I shoved the scissors, glue, and pickle jar under my bedspread.

Mom entered my room. She sniffed the air and said, "I smell sour pickles, old coffee, and glue."

I shrugged. "I don't smell anything."

Mom walked around my room, sniffing along the way. She said, "I came in to remind you to do your homework."

"Okay. I'll start it."

"What smells so bad in here?" she asked.

I shrugged again.

She finally left my room.

I reached under my bedspread to get the gluey pickle jar. But it was stuck. Glue had gotten all over my sheets and bedspread. I'd made a huge mess.

I finally pried out the jar. The glue had dried. The tissue paper wouldn't stick to the jar without more glue.

I squeezed the glue bottle. Nothing came out. I'd used up all the glue.

I threw the empty bottle in my trash can and put the jar in the back of my closet.

Mom walked into my room again and said, "Start your homework."

I nodded.

She looked at the glue bottle in my trash can. Then she sniffed again, walked over to my bed, reached under my bedspread, and felt my sheets. She said, "Ezekiel Heathcliff Meeks!"

I knew Mom was upset, because she'd called me by my full name.

"I'm upset!" she said.

I nodded again. "I know."

"You used glue in your room. You got it all over your sheets and bedspread," she said.

I nodded again. "I know."

Mom glared at me, which was another sign she was upset.

I felt guiltier than ever. The only thing I'd made for Mother's Day was a big mess.

THE HORROR of BUGS

and GRAMMAR WORKSHEETS

Bugs are bad, but
← bugs AND grammar
are worse!

When the bell rang for recess the next day, my classmates ran outside. I wanted to run with them. Instead, I stayed in the classroom.

I walked over to my teacher and said, "Can I talk to you?"

"May I," Mr. McNutty said.

"Huh?" I asked.

"May I talk to you."

"Oh. You want to talk to me too. That works out well," I said. "Can I talk first?"

Mr. McNutty shook his head. "That's not what I meant. I meant that the proper way to ask is, 'May I talk to you?' Not 'Can I talk to you?'."

"Please," I said.

"Please what?" Mr. McNutty asked.

"You forgot to say please," I said.

Mr. McNutty sighed. "What's up, Zeke?"

I took a deep breath. "I didn't make a Mother's Day card."

"Why not?" my teacher asked.

I was too embarrassed to tell him that I was scared of the bug on the card and that I had been mad at my mom.

So I ignored his question and asked, "Can I make the card today?"

"May I please make a card today?" said Mr. McNutty.

"You want to make a card for your mother too?" I asked.

He shook his head. "I meant that you should have used 'may' instead of 'can,' and you should have said 'please.'"

"Oh. Right. May I please make a Mother's Day card today?"

"Yes. You may make the card today," said Mr. McNutty.

"Thank you." I smiled. I could work on the card while my classmates did grammar worksheets, spelling practice, and other boring things.

"You may make the card in the classroom at lunchtime," Mr. McNutty said.

I frowned. Then I hurried outside to play at recess.

I had just reached the playground when the bell rang. Recess was over. I had to return to the classroom.

I spent the next few hours filling out grammar worksheets, practicing spelling, and doing other boring things.

When the lunch bell rang, everyone ran outside except Mr. McNutty and me.

I sat at my desk and looked out the window. The sun was shining and my best friend, Hector, was dribbling a basketball.

I sighed.

Mr. McNutty gave me supplies to make a Mother's Day card.

I heard laughter on the playground. I heard a ball dribbling. I heard Hector shout, "Great shot!"

I put my hands over my ears.

Then I wrote on the inside of the card, "Happy Mother's Day from your love bug. Love, Zeke." That was easy.

Next, I started making the bug for the outside of the card. That was scary. I tried to forget that the colored papers I was gluing onto the card were supposed to be a bug's body and wings. But I remembered. I tried to forget that bugs terrified me. I remembered that too.

I picked up the pipe cleaners. They looked just like bug antennae. I closed my eyes and glued them on.

"Why are your eyes closed?" Mr. McNutty asked me.

I shrugged.

"You just glued the bug's antennae onto the bug's bottom."

I opened my eyes. *Eek!* The bug's antennae were coming out of its butt. That made it look even scarier than a normal bug. I shook with fear.

"Are you okay?" Mr. McNutty asked me.

"Sure," I said. My voice quivered.

I took the pipe cleaner antennae off the bug's bottom and glued them onto its head.

"I'm done," I said. I wanted to get away from the awful bug. I also wanted to play basketball with Hector.

"You didn't decorate the bug's wings or put googly eyes on its head," Mr. McNutty said.

I frowned. "Oh, yeah."

I swiped a marker across the bug's wings a few times. Then I glued the eyes on the bug's head. I couldn't wait to escape from the terrifying bug and go outside with my friends. I said, "Now I'm done."

"No, you're not. Clean up," Mr. McNutty said.

I quickly cleaned up and put the Mother's Day card in the box under my desk. I asked my teacher, "Can I go outside now?"

"May you go outside now?" he corrected me.

"Yes I may," I said.

Then I ran to the playground.

Just as I got to the basketball court, the bell rang. I sighed and headed back to the classroom.

The Only Thing WORSE than a BUG Is ME

UN-Happy Mother's Day

Worst. Son. EVER.

When school let out on Friday, I needed to take home the bug card I'd made. But I was too scared to look at it. So I closed my eyes, reached into the box under my desk, pulled out the card, put it in my backpack, and zipped up the backpack. Once the scary bug card was out of sight, I opened my eyes.

When I got home, I whispered to my sister Alexa, "I have a great Mother's Day card for Mom."

"You don't need to whisper. Mom is in the backyard," Alexa said.

"Oh. I'll show you the card I made," I said loudly.

I closed my eyes again, slowly unzipped my backpack, and pulled out the card.

"That card is strange and ugly," Alexa said.

"Are you scared of the bug on it?" I asked.

She shook her head. "I don't see a bug on your card."

"Duh. There's a big, googly-eyed bug on the front of the card." I pointed at the card with my eyes squeezed tight. I was still too scared to open them.

"Zeke, there's no bug on that card," Alexa said.

She must have been trying to trick me.

As soon as I opened my eyes and looked, Alexa would probably say, "Ha-ha. Fooled you. Made you look. Of course there's a bug on that card."

"The only things on that card are weirdly shaped pipe cleaners, balled up paper, and a lot of glue," Alexa said.

I took a deep breath. I told myself to be brave. Then I opened my eyes and looked at the card.

Oh, no. I had grabbed the wrong card from the box under my desk. I'd taken the mean card I'd made a few days ago instead of the nice one I'd made today.

I opened the card and saw the mean words I'd written before: "The only thing worse than a bug is my mother."

I felt guiltier than ever now.

"This is the wrong card. I left my Mother's Day card at school by accident. I have to get it," I said.

"You can't get it in time. Mother's Day is Sunday. School is closed until Monday," Alexa said.

I groaned. "Now I won't have anything for Mom on Mother's Day."

Mia walked into the room and said, "Don't groan, Zeke. I'll cheer you up with a Princess Sing-Along song."

Oh, no. I put my hands over my ears.

But I still heard Mia's loud, screechy singing: "It's very rude to pick your nose, la la la. Or blow it like a fire hose, la la la."

"I'm not in the mood for silly songs," I said.

"It's a good thing Princess Sing-Along songs aren't silly. Are you in the mood for this one?" Mia asked. "Awesome gifts come from the heart, la la la. Awful gifts are burps and farts, la la la."

"No. I am not in the mood for that song either," I said.

"How about this one?"

Before Mia could start another song and destroy my ears, I shouted, "Stop!"

Mom ran in from the backyard. "Zeke, you sound very upset! Are you okay?"

"I was okay until Mia started singing," I said.

"What are you holding?" Mom pointed to the awful card in my hand.

"It's nothing," I said.

"It's probably a Mother's Day card," Mia said.

Mom smiled. "Aww! That's so nice, Zeke. I can't wait to get your card on Sunday. I bet it's really special."

Mom would lose that bet.

"I'm really looking forward to Mother's Day," she said.

I was really dreading it.

Things That Don't Exist:
PINOCCHIO,
PRINCESS SING-ALONG, and My
MOTHER'S DAY GIFT

See this guy? Doesn't exist.

On Saturday, only one day before Mother's Day, I still didn't have anything for my mom.

I walked into Alexa's room. She wore dark pink headphones. Yuck. She was sitting on her bed, staring at magazine pictures of teenage boys. Yuck. Posters of teenage boys hung on her wall. Yuck.

"Can I talk to you?" I asked.

Alexa lifted the right side of her headphones off her right ear. "You can talk. But I may not listen."

"I want to give Mom a Mother's Day gift. Do you have any ideas?" I asked.

Alexa didn't respond.

"Alexa," I said.

"What?"

"Do you have any ideas?" I asked again.

"Yes. My idea of a perfect boyfriend is a tall, blond guy with huge muscles and soft lips."

"Do you have any ideas for a Mother's Day gift?" I asked.

She took the right side of her headphones off her ear. "I could show you how to make Mom a beautiful scarf."

"That would be perfect," I said.

"Except it would take you weeks to make a scarf. And I used up all our yarn to make Mom a beautiful scarf myself," Alexa said.

"We could tell Mom that the scarf you made is a present from both of us," I said.

"No."

"Please?" I asked.

Alexa shook her head. Then she put her headphones back on and said, "I'm done listening to you."

"But, Alexa, I need —"

She cut me off. "Goodbye."

I sighed and walked out of her room.

I went to Mia's room next. She was sitting on her bed, holding a book called *100 Precious Pictures of Princess Sing-Along in Her Prettiest Princess Dresses*. Yuck. She was wearing her pink Princess Sing-Along hat. Yuck. A poster of Princess Sing-Along hung on Mia's wall. Yuck.

Mia sang, "Cover your mouth when you cough, la la la. So your hand will catch your glop, la la la." Yuck.

She ignored me. She screeched, "Nothing's worse than catching germs, la la la. Except eating snails and worms, la la la."

I moved closer to her and shouted, "Mia!"

She frowned and said, "Don't stand so close to me. I don't want to catch your bad germs. That would be almost as bad as eating snails or worms."

"I don't have bad germs. I'm not sick," I said.

Mia coughed in my face. "I have a cold. I hope you didn't catch my bad germs."

"Me, too." I backed away. Then I asked Mia, "What are you getting Mom for Mother's Day?"

"I made her a picture frame in preschool. My teacher said it's dazzling. She said I'm quite the artist."

"I'm not quite the artist. I'm quite *not* the artist. I tried to make a vase for Mom. Instead, I made a gluey, smelly mess," I said.

"Too bad," Mia said.

"Can we tell Mom that we both made the picture frame?" I asked.

"Do you want to me to lie to Mom?" Mia asked.

"Well, it's not exactly a —"

Before I could say the word "lie," Mia started singing another Princess Sing-Along song: "Don't lie like Pinocchio, la la la. Or your nose might grow and grow, la la la."

"Pinocchio isn't real. And neither is Princess Sing-Along," I said.

Mia put her hands on her hips and said, "Pinocchio and Princess Sing-Along are both very, very real. If we lie to Mom about the picture frame, our noses could grow and grow. I don't want my nose to grow and grow. It's perfect as it is, except for the snot stuck in it. That reminds me of another song."

I rushed out of Mia's room before she started picking her nose or singing about snotty noses or doing both those things at once.

"Alexa, Zeke, and Mia!" Mom called out. "I made special pancakes for you. I shaped them into hearts to show how much I love you."

Mother's Day was tomorrow, and I had nothing to show Mom I loved her. Not heart pancakes or a pretty vase or a nice card.

Not a beautiful scarf or a dazzling picture frame.

All I had for Mom was a goofy card and a gluey, smelly pickle jar.

I was the worst son ever.

MAJOR
Mother's Day
MESS

Imagine the biggest
mess you've ever seen.
This is WAY bigger.

I usually got up early on Sunday and watched *The Rotten Brats* and *The Moron Family* on TV.

But this Sunday morning was Mother's Day, and I had something better to do. I had decided to make Mom breakfast. Yesterday, she had cooked yummy pancakes for me. Today, I would make bacon, waffles, and coffee for her. I had never made breakfast before, but I'd seen my mom do it. It looked pretty easy.

I started with the coffee. First, I put a scoop of coffee into the coffee machine. Next, I poured a cup of water into the pot and then into the machine. Finally, I pressed the start button.

I heard the coffee brew. Making coffee had been as easy as pie. Actually, it was easier than pie, because I didn't know how to make pie.

Next, I opened the refrigerator to get the bacon. I didn't see any on the shelves. I opened every drawer in the fridge. No bacon. Uh-oh.

Maybe I could fry up something else, like ham or sausage. I looked in the refrigerator, but we didn't have those either.

The only meat I found was chicken lunchmeat. I decided to cook it like bacon. I put the lunchmeat in a pan and turned on the stove. The frying chicken lunchmeat looked kind of gross. It smelled *very* gross.

After a few minutes, I tried to turn over the chicken lunchmeat. But I couldn't. It was stuck to the pan. Uh-oh. I turned off the stove.

I hoped the waffles would turn out better. I looked for Mom's recipe. I opened almost every cupboard and drawer in the kitchen. Finally, I found the box of Mom's recipe cards and pulled out the waffle recipe.

I got out the ingredients and mixed them in
a bowl, turned on the waffle iron, and poured
in the batter. Making waffles was easy, except
for a few tiny problems:

1. Somehow the kitchen floor got coated
   with flour.

2. Somehow our dog did too.

3. I couldn't find the sugar.

4. I forgot to add butter.

5. I dropped an egg on the kitchen floor.

6. Eggshells got into the waffle batter.

7. A lot of the batter fell on the floor.

8. Our dog ate the batter on the floor and threw up.

Mom walked into the kitchen. She said, "Zeke, you aren't allowed to cook without a grown-up around."

"Now you're around," I said.

She looked at the open cupboards and drawers, the messy counter, and the floor full of flour, egg, and dog vomit. She frowned and said, "Ezekiel Heathcliff Meeks."

Uh-oh. Mom had used my full name. I quickly said, "Happy Mother's Day. I'm making breakfast for you. Sorry about the mess. I'll clean everything."

Mom stopped frowning.

"I wanted to surprise you," I said.

"You surprised me all right," Mom said. She didn't say it in a good way.

"Your special Mother's Day breakfast will be ready soon. Sit on the couch and relax," I said.

Mom went to the living room and sat down. She did not seem relaxed. She kept peering at the kitchen.

After a few minutes, I opened the waffle iron. The batter had stuck to its insides. Uh-oh.

I picked up a spatula and tried to remove the batter.

The spatula melted. Uh-oh.

"I smell burning rubber," Mom said as she hurried to the kitchen.

"The rubber spatula isn't working right," I said. It had melted into the waffles and the waffle iron. I'd ruined the waffles. I'd probably ruined the waffle iron, too.

"That spatula isn't supposed to get hot." Mom reached into a drawer and took out a different spatula.

"This is the one for hot things," she added.

Mom pointed to the pan on the stove. "What's that for?"

"I made fried chicken lunchmeat for you," I replied.

"Fried chicken lunchmeat?" Mom said. She didn't say it in a good way.

I took the spatula from Mom and tried to remove the lunchmeat from the pan. But it was still stuck. "I guess I should have used oil in the pan," I said.

Mom patted my head. "That's okay. I'm not hungry."

I wouldn't be hungry for burnt chicken lunchmeat stuck to a pan either.

"I bet you're thirsty for coffee," I said. I poured the coffee I'd made into a mug. A bunch of big, flaky coffee grounds fell into the mug too.

Mom frowned. "Did you put a filter in the coffee machine?"

"A filter? What's that?" I asked.

"It's thin paper that stops the coffee grounds from getting into the coffee."

I sighed. "Oh. I guess I ruined the coffee too."

"You tried your best," Mom said. "Clean up the mess in the kitchen, please."

It took me a long time to sponge off the counters, clean the coffeemaker and frying pan, throw away the melted spatula and ruined waffle iron, and wash the kitchen floor.

"Sorry your Mother's Day breakfast turned out so bad," I told Mom.

"That's all right. I'm glad you made me a card," she said.

I shook my head. "I left it at school."

"What about the card I saw you holding on Friday?" she asked.

"I made that when I was goofing off. I made a nice Mother's Day card later, but I took the wrong one home."

"Well, I'm excited to see the gift you made for me."

"It turned out as well as today's breakfast. I'll get it." I fetched the gluey, smelly pickle jar from my bedroom closet and showed it to my mom.

She plugged her nose.

"Sorry. I tried to make a vase. Happy
Mother's Day," I said. Then I threw the jar into
the kitchen trash can.

"Thank you," Mom said, still plugging her
nose. "I'll make breakfast."

"Do you want me to help?" I asked.

She glanced at the awful pickle jar, ruined waffle iron, and melted spatula in the trash can. She looked at our flour-covered dog. Then she frowned, shook her head a bunch of times, and said, "No, thank you."

The PRESENCE of the PRESENTS

Don't be fooled by nice wrapping.

Mom made scrambled eggs and fried potatoes for everyone. The kitchen counters and floors stayed clean, no machines or utensils got ruined, and the food smelled great.

I ate a forkful of eggs and potatoes and said, "This is delicious, Mom."

"Yeah. Happy Mother's Day," Alexa said.

Mia sang in her screechy voice: "On Mother's Day we celebrate, la la la, our mommies who are super great, la la la. They bandage their children's cuts, la la la, and wipe babies' poopy butts, la la la."

I put my fork down. I couldn't eat after hearing about poopy butts.

"Mom shouldn't have to do chores on Mother's Day," Alexa said. "So Zeke will clean up after breakfast."

"Me?" I asked.

"Thanks for agreeing to do it, Zeke," Alexa said.

For the second time that morning, I washed dishes and cleaned the kitchen.

After I finished, we all went to the living room. Alexa handed Mom a present and said, "You'll love this."

Mom opened it. It was a bumpy, scratchy scarf in a horrible shade of green. It looked like leftover pea soup that had been barfed up. I knew what that looked like because I'd recently eaten leftover pea soup and barfed it up. In summary, the scarf was very, very ugly.

Mom smiled anyway. She said, "I love your gift, Alexa. I can tell you worked really hard on it. It's wonderful."

It was more like the opposite of wonderful. Un-wonderful or wonder-less or wonder-not or whatever the word was.

Mia gave Mom a present next. She said, "You'll love my gift too. It took me about a jillion hundred and ninety ten ton hours to make."

"That's a lot of hours," Mom said as she opened the gift.

Mia had made a picture frame from dirty popsicle sticks and a huge amount of glue. The frame was crooked and splinters stuck out of it.

"It's perfect," Mom said.

Perfectly awful, I thought.

"Alexa, Mia, and Zeke, you sure made this a great Mother's Day," Mom said.

I shook my head. "Not me. All I gave you was a ruined breakfast and a stinky pickle jar."

"You gave me your time and effort. You tried hard to make me breakfast and a vase. That shows you really care."

The phone rang. Mom answered it. She smiled and said, "Kids, your father is on the line. I'm putting him on speaker phone."

Dad said over the phone, "I hope you're all treating your mother well today."

"They're treating me very well," Mom said. Then she took Dad off speaker and talked to him in private.

We each got a turn to speak to Dad. I sat on the couch and told him about the smelly, gluey vase and the disgusting breakfast I'd made.

He started laughing, which made me laugh too. My Mother's Day projects had seemed terrible at the time, but now they seemed funny.

After the phone call, Mom said, "Talking to your Dad was a great gift for me."

"Me, too," I said. "Although an even greater gift would be talking to Dad while he was buying me a new video game."

Mom smiled.

Alexa sat next to me on the couch. She opened a bag and pulled out knitting needles and a ball of scratchy yarn.

The yarn was the color of runny diarrhea. I knew what color runny diarrhea was because I'd had it a few weeks ago.

"What are you knitting now?" I asked.

"A scarf like the one I gave Mom. But this one will be brown," Alexa said. "It's for your birthday, Zeke."

That disgusting scarf was for me? *Ugh.*

But I guess it was nice of Alexa to make me a gift. Her birthday was coming up. I'd make her a gluey, smelly pickle jar vase.

Alexa turned on the TV, flipped through the channels, and stopped on a show called *Adorable Teen Boys and the Girls Who Want to Smooch Them.*

Mia joined us in the living room and said, "Smooching reminds me of a Princess Sing-Along song. Once the next commercial comes on, I'll sing it for everyone."

"It's terrific to be with you kids. I couldn't ask for a better gift for Mother's Day," Mom said.

I didn't think being with Alexa and Mia was terrific. I didn't even think it was good. I could ask for a hundred gifts better than watching awful TV shows and listening to horrible Princess Sing-Along songs during the commercials.

"Happy Mother's Day," I told Mom again with a big hug.

Then I hurried to my bedroom.

ABOUT THE AUTHOR

D. L. Green lives in California with her husband, three children, silly dog, and a big collection of rubber chickens. She loves to read, write, and joke around.

ABOUT THE ILLUSTRATOR

Josh Alves is very thankful for all the support and encouragement his mom has given him! He gets to draw in Maine, where he lives with his wonderful wife and their four creative kids.

WHY DO MOMS MAKE US SO MAD SOMETIMES?
(And other really important questions)

Write answers to these questions, or discuss them with your friends and classmates.

1. Why do moms make their kids so mad sometimes? Have you ever gotten really mad at your mom? How did you get over it?

2. Both my card and my vase were crafting disasters! How would you have done things differently to make them turn out better?

3. What are the three coolest things about your mom?

4. If I could have given my mom any gift in the world, I would have brought Dad home for the day. What gift would you give your mom if you could choose anything?

BIG WORDS
according to Zeke

TRY USING THEM IN SENTENCES JUST LIKE I DO

<u>ALLOWANCE:</u> The money you get from your parents, usually for helping out around the house.

<u>AMAZING:</u> Things that are amazing make you VERY happy. A free day at Thrillsville Amusement Park would be amazing, for example.

<u>ANTENNAE:</u> You seriously are going to make me think about antennae? Okay, fine. They're the super creepy, skinny little things that stick out of a bug's head.

<u>AROMA:</u> A nice or tasty smell. What I wouldn't give to come across cookie aroma right now!

<u>AWESOME:</u> Really, super great. Awesome things include getting a new video game and having school canceled unexpectedly.

<u>DAZZLING:</u> When something is so fantastic, it makes you forget what you're doing and keeps all of your attention.

<u>DELICIOUS:</u> Tasting great, like brownies, marshmallows, and ice cream.

<u>DIARRHEA:</u> It's when you have to go to the bathroom a lot and what comes out is brown and watery. It is also SUPER gross.

These scary pointy things are antennae.

DISEASE: Something awful that makes people feel sick and tired.

DISGUSTING: Things that make you go, "EW!" like Princess Sing-Along, most girls, and every bug known to man.

EXTREMELY: Super-duper, very much so.

GUILTY: That gross feeling you get when you know that you were bad.

INSULT: To say or do something that made a person feel bad. Note: I said a PERSON, not Princess Sing-Along.

MOSQUITO: A tiny, but terrifying, bug that is awful because it takes your blood and leaves you with an itchy bump in return.

QUIVER: A fancier word for the word "shake."

SCREECHY: Loud and high-pitched and awful! In other words, everything that has to do with Princess Sing-Along.

UTENSILS: Spoons, forks, spatulas, knives, and other handy tools you use to cook and eat with.

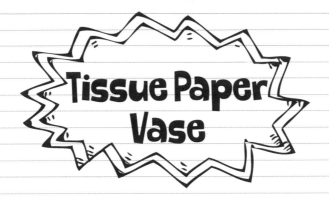

Tissue Paper Vase

I know that I messed up big time on my mom's vase. But it wasn't because it was a bad idea. I just didn't follow the directions very well. Well, here's your chance to make a nice gift for someone. Don't let my awful vase fool you — this could actually turn out pretty cool!

What you need:

- a clean, dry glass jar

- tissue paper in a few different colors

- scissors

- white craft glue

- bowl

- water

- foam craft brush

What you do:

1. Cut the paper into small pieces. You might want to cut it into different shapes and sizes or cut it all the same. You decide.

2. Mix the glue with a little water in the bowl. Use just enough water so that it is easy to paint over the tissue paper.

3. Brush the glue mixture on part of the jar. Then place some cut tissue paper on the glue. Gently press the paper in place and then brush a little of the glue mixture over it. Continue to cover the rest of the jar in the same way, including the bottom.

4. When the whole jar is covered, stand it on its mouth and brush the entire outside with the glue mixture. Let dry completely. To completely seal the jar, repeat with a few more layers of the glue mixture. Be sure to let the jar dry between each layer.

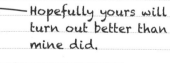

← Hopefully yours will turn out better than mine did.

Zeke Meeks

AHHHH! Finished reading and want more Zeke?

Have no fear!
The coolest guy you'll ever meet has lots of awesome stories to share.

www.capstonepub.com

AWESOME HAIR

CHARMING SMILE

Zeke Meeks

COOLEST THIRD
GRADER YOU'LL
EVER MEET!